D0350473

ACCOLADES FOR THE
ALDO ZELNICK COMIC NOVEL SERIES

An alphabetical adventure for middle-grade readers 7 to 13

Book of the Year Award, juvenile fiction, *ForeWord Reviews*

Colorado Book Award, juvenile literature

Mountains & Plains Independent Booksellers
Association Regional Book Award

Creative Child magazine Seal of Excellence

Kids' Next Indiebound selection

Independent Publisher Silver "IPPY" Award

Creative Child magazine Preferred Choice Award

Quid Novi Award, first prize

Moonbeam Children's Book Award, silver medal for comic/graphic novel

Top 10 Educational Children's Products - Dr. Toy

Book of the Year Award, kids' fiction, *Creative Child* magazine

WHAT READERS ARE SAYING:
(kid comments are in Aldo's handwriting)

"It was the funniest book I have ever read.
The illustrations are hilarious. It is better than
Diary of a Wimpy Kid."
— Tavis

"The Aldo Zelnick books keep getting better and better."
— Mary Lee Hahn, teacher and readingyear.blogspot.com blogger

"You will laugh out loud—I guarantee it. The books are THAT funny."
— Becky Bilby, inthepages.blogspot.com

"I've been waiting for a series to come along that could knock Wimpy Kid off its pedastel as the most popular series in my library. Well, this may be it: the Aldo Zelnick Comic Novels. Save room on your shelves for 26 volumes!"
— Donna Dannenmiller, elementary librarian

"Aldo is pretty awesome in my book."
— Dr. Sharon Pajka, English professor, Gallaudet University

"The other night I caught my 8-year-old twins giggling on the living room couch as they took turns reading *Artsy-Fartsy* aloud to each other. Then one morning I found it on their nightstand with a headlamp resting on the cover from the previous night's under-cover reading. That's a true badge of honor in this house. You hit this one out of the park."
— Becky Jensen

"As a teacher of 20 years I have never come across a book that has engaged readers so intensely so quickly. The boys in my reading group devoured the series and were sad when they finished the most recent one."
— Cheryl Weber, Director of Educational Support, Indian Community School

"One of the most remarkable things about these books is the voice of Aldo, which rings true from every page. The hilarious drawings enhance the text with jokes and visual humor that make Aldo's personality pop."
— Rebecca McGregor, Picture Literacy

"THE BOOK WAS VERY HILARIOUS. IT MADE US LAUGH OUT LOUD. YOU HAVE THE BEST CHARACTERS EVER!"
— Sebastian

"We recommend A is for Aldo! Hilarious stories, goofy drawings, and even sneaky new vocabulary words. If you are an admirer of *Diary of a Wimpy Kid*, you'll adore Aldo Zelnick."
— Oak Park Public Library

"I LOVE the Aldo Zelnick books so much that I want to read them for the rest of my life!"
— Gregory, age 9

"This terrific series will be enjoyed by all readers and constantly in demand. Highly recommended."
— South Sound Book Review Council of Washington libraries

"This is a fun series that my students adore."
— Katherine Sokolowski, 5th grade teacher

"Every library that serves Wimpy Kid fans (which, honestly, is every library period) should have the Aldo Zelnick series on its shelves."
— Katie Ahearn, children's librarian, Washington DC

"Aldo is an endearing narrator. His deadpan sense of humor is enjoyable even for adults. Each book is a fast-paced, light read, perfect for the kid looking for a transition from comics to chapter books."
— Sarah, children's buyer, Left Bank Books

"When I am reading an Aldo Zelnick book in RTI, I don't want to go back to my classroom. Somehow I want to keep reading...and I don't like reading."
— an elementary student

"I am completely charmed by this series. The drawings and text have the quality of simultaneously being appealing to children and also amusing for adults. A big strength here is in the development of the characters. This is wonderful, since this is going to be an A to Z series and we'll have plenty of time to get to know them better. These are individuals with staying power. With the sketchbook comes a wonderful, not-overstated message of allowing Aldo to be himself and follow his creativity. Bravo!"
— Jean Hanson

"...a must for your elementary school reader."
— Christy, Reader's Cove bookstore

"In the wake of Wimpy Kid and Amelia's Notebooks comes Aldo Zelnick. Oceanak has created a funny and lively hero. The illustrations add to the humor."
— *Library Media Connection*

Hotdogger

AN ALDO ZELNICK COMIC NOVEL

Written by Karla Oceanak

Illustrated by Kendra Spanjer

BAILIWICK PRESS

Also by Karla Oceanak
and Kendra Spanjer —
Artsy-Fartsy, Bogus,
Cahoots, Dumbstruck,
Egghead, Finicky, Glitch,
All Me, All the Time

This is a work of fiction. Names, characters, places, and incidents are either the product of the author's imagination or are used fictitiously. Any resemblance to actual persons, living or dead, events, or locales is entirely coincidental.

Copyright © 2013 by Karla Oceanak and Kendra Spanjer

All rights reserved. No part of this publication may be reproduced, stored in a retrieval system, or transmitted in any form or by any means, electronic, mechanical, photocopying, or otherwise, without the prior written permission of the publisher.

Published by:
Bailiwick Press
309 East Mulberry Street
Fort Collins, Colorado 80524
(970) 672-4878
Fax: (970) 672-4731
www.bailiwickpress.com
www.aldozelnick.com

Manufactured by:
Friesens Corporation, Altona, Canada
June 2013
Job # 85863

Book design by:
Launie Parry
Red Letter Creative
www.red-letter-creative.com

ISBN 978-1-934649-37-4

Library of Congress Control Number: 2013909424

22 21 20 19 18 17 16 15 14 13   7 6 5 4 3 2 1

Dear Aldo —
Hunker down.*
That's what
January's for!
(At least until
it's time to
hit the slopes*...)
Goosy

ALDO,

We come nearest to
the great when we are
great in _humility_.*

— Mr. Mot

WHO'S WHO

ME – ALDO ZELNICK. SKIER OR NON-SKIER? THAT IS THE QUESTION.

TIMOTHY, HOCKEY (AND ALL SPORTS) HOTDOGGER.*

MY BEST FRIEND, JACK.

MY GRANDMA, GOOSY. SNOWBOARDER AND HULA GIRL.

MR. MOT, NEIGHBOR, SURFER, AND HAWAII AFICIONADO.

THE REST OF MY FAMILY: MOM, DAD, AND OUR DOG, MAX.

HERCULES. POOP-SCOOPING HERO.

JACK'S DAD, FRITZ, AND HIS NEW "FRIEND," HAZEL.

JACK'S STINKY DOG, SLATE.

MY OTHER FRIENDS, BEE AND TOMMY GELLER AND DANNY.

BACON BOY, LETTUCE LADY AND TORMADO, THE STARS OF MY VERY OWN COMICS.

MR. KRUG, MY 5TH GRADE TEACHER, AND MR. FODDER, MY CAFETERIA GUY.

THIS ALDO ZELNICK KID MAKES THESE SKETCHBOOK STORIES.

EVEN THOUGH I'M CUTER THAN KITTENS, I HAD TO WAIT FOR THE H BOOK TO MAKE AN APPEARANCE. (DO YOU KNOW WHY?)

ANYWAY, I'M HERE TO TELL YOU THAT WHEN YOU SEE *, IT MEANS YOU CAN LOOK IN THE WORD GALLERY AT THE BACK OF THE BOOK TO SEE WHAT THE WORD MEANS.

HOTDOGGER

GLITCH

FINICKY

EGGHEAD

DUMBSTRUCK

CAHOOTS

BOGUS!

ARTSY-FARTSY

THE WIMPIEST KID

"You try this, Aldo," said Timothy. "I dare you."

One thing you need to know about my super-jock 15-year-old brother is that he's constantly daring me to do something athletic. Which is SO annoying! But today it was uber annoying because he had invaded our winter fort headquarters* (A.K.A. my bedroom closet) and was hanging over our heads like Spider Man—but without the awesomeness.

"I dare <u>you</u> not to be so dumb," I said.

"You <u>can't</u> do this," he said.

"I don't <u>want</u> to do that," I said.

"Can you believe Christmas break is over and we have to go back to school tomorrow?" said Jack. He's my best friend, but he's also a subject-changer. Whenever a conversation gets even a little bit heated,* he says something random to try to trick everyone into being amiable.

"Finally!" cried Bee. "I miss school!"

"Oh please!" I said. "And now it's January, which is <u>THE</u> MOST HUMDRUM* month of the entire year. *Gah.* <u>Nothing</u> fun ever happens in January."

Timothy grabbed the top of the doorway and swung himself over my head and out of the closet. Before I could stop them, my eyeballs raced backward to see his landing, and I tipped over onto my back.

"Nothing fun except for skiing!" he howled. He bent his knees, leaned forward a little, tucked his fists up near his armpits, then hopped side-to-side in a pretend-skiing motion. "Aldo, did you know we Zelnicks get to go skiing in a couple weeks?" he asked.

My heart sank through my chest and out onto the floor, where it landed with a thud.

I <u>hate</u> skiing. My parents made me go a couple times when I was little, and I <u>stink</u> at it! But in Colorado, where I live, all the 5th graders in the whole state get to ski for free, and the rest of my family is ski-crazy...so I should have known this day was coming.

"Ugggh," I pointed out. "Skiing is the <u>worst</u>."

"You're such a wimp!" said Timothy. "How come my brother has to be the wimpiest kid in the world?!" And he slammed the closet door, leaving me and Jack and Bee in the dark.

"Actually, I think there are at least a couple kids in our school wimpier than you," came a voice out of the blackness. It was Jack. He was trying to make me feel better.

"I've got it!" said a second voice. "Let's try some activities we've never tried before." It was Bee. She was trying to make January more interesting.

"At least there's video games," said a third voice. It was me. I was trying to be realistic.

I opened the fort door, and we shuffled out to play Heavenly Sword until Dad called me to dinner and Jack and Bee went home.

p.s. Today was so humdrum I squirted a mustard message onto my hot dog:

BACON BOY IN
OH SAY...CAN YOU SKI?

☐ WATER SKI?

☐ JET SKI?

☐ CROSS-COUNTRY SKI?

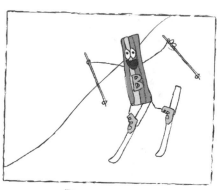

☐ DOWNHILL SKI?

☐ SNOWBOARD?

☒ WATCH SKIING?

SURVEY COMPLETED BY ALDO ZELNICK. (IN CASE YOU DIDN'T KNOW.)

DENTAL HYGIENE*

So there I was at the dentist today, chillaxing in the chair you lie down on (well, chillaxing as much as you can with a light like the sun shining in your face and miniature metal tools attacking your teeth). The tooth-cleaner lady was asking me how my Christmas vacation went, and I was trying to remember, since it already seemed like ancient history.

(Have you ever noticed that the tooth-cleaner lady always asks you a question right when her tools are in the way of your tongue answering? Sheesh.)

Anyways, before I could respond, I broke out in a heavy-duty* case of the hiccups. Open-mouth hiccups are infinity times louder than regular shut-mouth ones. I'm serious! Try it sometime!

At first my hiccups made the tooth-cleaner lady giggle. Then she tried to stop them. She used her water-squirter thingy to shoot some H_2O* into my mouth and told me to swallow, but the hiccups kept on coming. So she kept on cleaning! And I kept on lying there in hiccupy humiliation.*

I stared up at the ceiling. They'd taped a poster there that's supposed to distract you from the weirdness of a stranger having her hands inside your mouth for an hour.

It was a picture of a white sandy beach (wait...aren't all beaches sandy?) with a few coconut trees along the edge. The sky was Smurf blue, and the water was the color of an aquamarine crayon. A capital C of a wave rolled toward the beach, and inside the C rode a guy on an orange surfboard. His knees were bent and his arms stuck out and his smile gleamed with white teeth.

At the top of the poster was a single word in flowery letters:

Hawaii

COLOR KEY:

WONDER BREAD LEATHER BOOT SMURF AQUA-MARINE TURQUOISE SAPPHIRE BLUE

From the chair-bed dealie I was lying on, I could also swivel my eyes to look out the window, where the Colorado winter ice and wind battled each other to see who was the most evil.

I've never been to Hawaii, but it sure looked like heaven-on-earth from where I sat.

8 WAYS TO HALT* THE HICCUPS

I still had the hiccups when I got home from the dentist! So I tried these cures, which are supposed to work, according to the internet:

1. Eat a spoonful of sugar. If you still have the hiccups, eat another spoonful. Repeat as long as possible because this is probably the only time your mom will let you eat straight from the sugar bowl.

2. Stand on your head and drink a glass of water upside-down. Try not to get water in your nose holes.

3. Hold your breath as long as you can.

4. Breathe into a paper bag.

5. Stick your fingers in your ears. (Pretty sure this one is bogus and is just trying to make you look like a doofus...but I tried it anyway.)

6. Ask someone to scare you. (Kind of defeats the purpose, doesn't it?)

7. Stick out your tongue, grab it with your fingers, and pull. (Ew. Tongues are horrid.*)

8. Tickle your mouth ceiling with a Q-tip. (Ew. Putting cotton in my mouth gives me the heebie-jeebies.*)

NEVER AGAIN.

Number 8 <u>finally</u> did the trick, making it possible for me to enjoy a huge helping* of honey-baked ham at dinner. Yorm!

p.s. Despite all the excitement of dentistry and hiccups, today was so humdrum that I counted the hairs in my left eyebrow. 309. Then I counted the right: 287. Ack! All these years my whole face has been out of balance and no one even told me!

MY LEFT EYEBROW IS ON <u>YOUR</u> RIGHT...

MY RIGHT EYEBROW IS PRACTICALLY BALD.

THIS GUY IS TRYING TO HELP EVEN THINGS OUT. THANKS, BUDDY.

THIS EYEBROW IS SO HIRSUTE* I THINK I'LL NAME IT HARRY.

I CAN'T HACK* IT!

At lunch recess today I was standing in my usual standing spot on the playground, zoning out. You know how sometimes your body can be somewhere but your mind can be somewhere else? Well, my mind was skiing. I mean, it was thinking about skiing and wondering how it could get me out of having to go, when for no reason, Bee threw something at me. It hit me on my side-butt and fell to the ground.

SERIOUSLY. HOW DO BOYS EVER BECOME MEN?

I THINK THEREFORE I DON'T SKI!

"Hey! You can't just huck* stuff at people!" I said.

"It's a hacky sack," she said,
reaching down to pick it up.

It was the size of
a clementine orange, and it
was red and white and squooshy.
"You kick it."

She picked it up, tossed it into the
air right next to herself, then stuck her
foot out and kicked it in my direction.

I caught it in my left hand.
"Hey, I just caught a ball-like object,"
I said. (I'm not usually so pro at
ball-catching.)

"No hands,"
said Miss It's-January-So-
Let's-Try-Some-New-Activities.
"Just feet and legs."

So I lobbed the hacky sack toward Danny, and he stepped forward and bumped it up into the air with his knee. Then it dropped near his foot, and he toe-kicked it over to Jack.

"Nice kick, Danny!" said Bee all girlishly.

"He can't hear you," I reminded her. Danny's deaf. Meanwhile, Danny was keeping the hacky sack in the air all by himself with knee bounces and toe flicks.

"I showed him the hacky sack when we were eating lunch, and he signed to me that he'd never played before," said Bee. "But he's awesome!"

He _is_ awesome, I thought. But he doesn't have to be such a show-off about it.

"He's not a show-off. He's just giving it some effort," said Bee in a huffy* voice. "You should try it sometime."

Oops. Guess I said that out loud.

After recess came the neverending joys of math, science, and history. Then Jack and I slip-slided home on the January ice.

p.s. Today was so boring that when I got home from school, I stretched out on the floor in front of the heat vent and tried to see how many seconds I could go without blinking while hot furnace air blew onto my eyeballs. The answer: 8 long, miserable seconds.

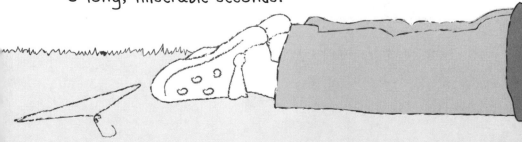

p.p.s. Timothy just got home from hockey practice and showed me a YouTube video of a guy on skis going down a steep, snowy mountain—which is horrible enough, but this guy also had an avalanche chasing behind him.

WHY IT'S JUST NOT POSSIBLE FOR ME TO GO SKIING

1. I'm not good at activities that involve balancing and moving at the same time. This is a hard, cold fact, just like Pluto is not a planet and Timothy is in love with anything that involves chasing a ball around like a nitwit.

2. I'm acrophobic. (That means afraid of heights.)

3. Last time I went skiing, about 100 toddlers zoomed past me. (See page 60.)

4. My snowpants don't fit.

5. When I fall down on skis, it's impossible to get back up. I could <u>die</u> lying there!

6. I get headaches at high altitudes, especially when I eat the snow.

7. Skiing is just plain not natural. How many other creatures strap slippery boards to their feet then head down a mountainside? Exactly!

8. I honor* and celebrate my unique specialness. Skiing is <u>not</u> part of my unique specialness... and that's OK.

THEY SAVED
THE BEST STATE
FOR LAST

WHAT'S HAIRY, BROWN, AND WEARS SUNGLASSES?

A COCONUT ON VACATION!

OR A DOG WHO THINKS HE'S HIP. *

Mr. Mot came to our house after dinner tonight to play guitar with my dad. As usual, he had on a Hawaiian shirt under his winter coat. It's like his old-guy uniform or something. Anyways, it reminded me of that entrancing beach poster on the ceiling at the dentist's office.

So I tugged on the bottom of Mr. Mot's Hawaiian shirt and asked, "Have you ever been here?"

He looked at me like I had three heads—and at least one of the heads was an alien and one had a boogy-nose.

29

There was a long pause. "Why, of course...," he finally said. "I have had the pleasure of being a visitor in the Zelnick home on <u>many</u> an occasion! Are you feeling well, Aldo?"

"No! Not <u>here</u>. <u>Hawaii</u>! Have you ever been to <u>Hawaii</u>?" Sheesh. Sometimes you have to talk to old people like they're really young people.

"Oh! Why, yes! The Aloha State is a favorite destination of mine. I am exceedingly fortunate to have a brother with a condominium near Hanuama Bay."

"Coooool... Is it as awesome as it looks in the pictures?" By now I was sitting down at our computer and Googling Hawaii images. Up came a screenful of blueness—blue water and blue skies and white stripes of sand, garnished with green coconut trees here and there.

"Ah, Hawaii," sighed Mr. Mot. He stood behind me so he could see the computer screen too. "It is the very definition of halcyon*—peaceful and calm. Ideal weather. Lovely beyond words." He pointed at one of the pictures. "Why, that is Hanuama Bay! I learned to snorkel there and came face-to-face with a *honu*—a sea turtle."

TURTLE-OO!

"Did he bite you?"

"Sea turtles are gentle creatures. He merely waved at me and swam past."

"Pretty sure turtles don't gesture. Did you ride one of these water skateboards too?"

"Oh yes. Surfing is like poetry in motion. And you know how much I love poetry."

Now it was <u>my</u> turn to sigh. "Hawaii is so amazing!" I realized out loud. "How come I have to live here in Colorado, where it's cold and boring? And there's skiing instead of surfing? Geez. My parents picked the worst state in the country!"

"There you are wrong, my young friend. You and I are fortunate to live in the heavenly Rocky Mountains." Mr. Mot turned to go find my dad. "Yet I fully understand your use of hyperbole* to express your impatience for warmer weather..."

He went on like that as he walked away, but I don't know what other hot air* came out of his mouth because I turned my attention back to the computer screen to learn more about the Best. State. Ever!

HAWAII, WHERE HAVE YOU BEEN HIDING ALL MY LIFE?

NIIHAU

KAUAI

Hawaii

(THE STATE THAT'S ACTUALLY A COLLECTION OF 8 ISLANDS!)

FUN FACTS:

- THE LAST OF THE 50 STATES TO JOIN THE USA

- ABOUT 3,600 MILES FROM MY HOUSE

- ONLY 12 LETTERS IN THE HAWAIIAN ALPHABET:
  A, E, I, O, U, H, K, L, M, N, P, W

- THE HAWAIIAN ISLANDS ARE ACTUALLY THE VERY TIP-TOPS OF GIANT MOUNTAINS ON THE OCEAN FLOOR. (WEIRD! I LIVE BY MOUNTAINS AND HAWAII IS ALSO MOUNTAINS! HAWAII MOUNTAINS ARE THE SNOW-LESS VOLCANO KIND, UNLIKE OURS.)

- ALOHA IS A HAWAIIAN WORD THAT MEANS HELLO **AND** GOODBYE (HOW ARE YOU SUPPOSED TO KNOW IF SOMEONE'S COMING OR GOING?)

OAHU

Honolulu

NORTH

MOLOKAI

LANAI

KAHOOLAWE

MAUI

= volcano top

HAWAII

p.s. Today was so humdrum that after I finished drawing Hawaii, I snuck my dad's ironing board into my room so I could try surfing. You know, in case Mr. Mot invites me to go to Hawaii with him any day now.

THESE HIEROGLYPHICS* PROBABLY SAY:

HANDLE WITH CARE! THIS GAUDY VASE WILL BE WORTH $MILLIONS$ IN 2,500 YEARS!

HERCULES!

Mr. Krug, my 5th grade teacher, is teaching us Greek myths. Today he started Hercules.

Usually I'm "who cares" about super-jocks like my brother, but Hercules? He did way cooler things with his athletic-ness. Everybody knows that he was this uber strong Greek hero guy who was half-man/half-god, but <u>not</u> everybody knows that he had to do a bunch of really hard chores to make up for a mistake he made.

(Um, yeah. It was a pretty bad mistake. He shot his own kids with a bow-and-arrow. But he did it because this crazy goddess lady named Hera cast a stronger-than-Voldemort spell on him, so he was basically innocent by reason of mythology.)

Anyways, Hercules had to do 12 impossible tasks called "labors."

"Hercules' first labor was to slay the Nemean lion!" roared Mr. Krug.

MR. KRUG LIKES TO ACT THINGS OUT. HE SAYS IT KEEPS EVERYONE AWAKE, BUT BEWARE IF YOU'RE SITTING IN THE SPIT ZONE.

RAWR!!!

"This lion was enchanted by evil," he continued. "It had been killing the innocent townspeople of Nemea. Hercules shot his bow at the lion, but the arrow just bounced off its magical fur. So he had to sneak into the lion's cave and wrestle it with his own bare hands! It was an epic fight. Even though the lion bit off one of his fingers, Hercules won. The mighty Nemean lion lay conquered at his feet."

THAT TEACHER IS SCARY! AND THAT FINGER—BLECH!

I MISS BILL ALREADY.

HEY NEW GUYS! GET YOUR HEADS IN THE GAME.

Hercules's second labor was to kill the hydra, which was this snake-beast with tons of heads. Every head had a mouth full of deadly fangs. Whenever Hercules chopped off a head, <u>two more</u> heads grew back! I hate when that happens! The secret was that <u>one</u> of the hydra's heads made it immortal, so when Hercules figured that out and sliced off the special head with a golden sword—*bam*. Cross chore number 2 off the to-do list.

The last Hercules task we learned about today was the third one: catching a super-fast deer. For <u>1 whole year</u> he chased it around Greece and some other countries. Finally, one night when it was asleep, he trapped it in a net.

Sheesh. I don't know which is worse— risking your life fighting deadly beasts or having to <u>run</u> every day for an entire year.

Jack came over after school, and we played Hercules and the lion. (We agreed we could pretend until we're in middle school—as long it's superhero-type fighting and Timothy doesn't see us.) Jack wanted to be Hercules, but I told him the huskiness of my body looks more muscle-y. He said my hair looks lionish. He had a point there, I had to admit, so we switched back and forth. Then, since it was Friday night, we split a frozen pizza and watched this old cartoon on Netflix called Hey Arnold!.

p.s. Even <u>with</u> Hercules and pizza and Hey Arnold!, today was so humdrum that Jack and I also ended up teaching ourselves to do headstands. It was hard, but we kept trying until we could balance for 5 seconds without falling over. (Leaning against a wall, of course. Nobody except those Cirque du Soleil guys can do it without a wall.)

SCHMOPANTS

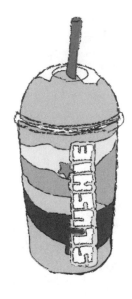

According to the internet, an Icee is basically the same thing as a Slushie, except Icees have carbonation bubbles mixed in.

Aha! So THAT'S WHY they make me burp!

My mom sprung a sneak shopping attack on me today.

Everybody knows that Saturday mornings are for nothing-doing, but Mom said I had to go to Target with her to "pick up a few things."

Gah. I should have known better. But sometimes at Target she lets me buy Yu-Gi-Oh cards, so I didn't even put up a fight. Instead, I walked right into her trap.

She bought me an Icee (red flag!) then herded*
me over to the clothes area of doom.

She ambled through the racks, touching all the shirts and calling the hoodies* "cute." Then...

"How about these?" she said all innocent-like.

"Nah. I'm good."

The realizing that this Target trip was to get me ready for skiing was dawning on me all at once, like a Hawaii sunrise. So I sucked up the rest of my Icee in one hasty* suck.

"Owww!" I cried. I bowed my head and put my hand to my forehead. Yup, I had just given myself a brain freeze. On purpose.

"What's wrong?" My mom is hard to hoodwink,* but if she has a weakness, it's kids in pain. This is a useful fact.

"Headache," I moaned. "Bad headache."

So she hung up the snowpants and walked me over to the nearest bench. After we sat there for a minute or two and I had thought up Plan B, I told her I was feeling better (which I was, since ice-cream headaches only last a few seconds) and I was ready to pick out shampoo.

"I hear Herbal Essences has some good new smells," I said. This was meant to be a red herring.*

"All right...," she said. "We'll stop by the hair products aisle...after you try on snowpants."

"But...snowpants make my butt look big!" This was meant to be a mom-sympathy herring.

"Don't be silly. We're going skiing next weekend, and your old snowpants are too small."

It was time to turn to my Why I Can't Go Skiing list. Only I didn't have this sketchbook with me, so I had to flip to it in my mind.

"I know!" I announced. "I'm afraid of heights!"

"Good thing your feet are on the ground when you ski," she said as she began pushing the shopping cart away.

"But what about the chairlift?" I was following her now, and we were headed due snowpants.

Oops.

CHAIRLIFTS CARRY YOU UP THE MOUNTAIN BECAUSE IT'S FUN TO HURTLE* YOURSELF DOWN THE MOUNTAIN. YEAH, RIGHT.

"I suppose you can stay on the kids' hill and use the magic carpet lift."

"What's that?"

"It's like a moving sidewalk. You just stand on it and it carries you up."

"Oh." That sounded kinda cool. I didn't realize it until that moment, but I've always <u>wanted</u> a moving sidewalk that would carry me around. Which is what I was thinking about when I felt Mom tugging snowpants up <u>over my sweatpants!</u>, right there in the boys' clothes section.

MOM!!! STOP DRESSING ME IN PUBLIC!

GLADLY. <u>YOU</u> FINISH.

The snowpants fit OK, and the next thing I knew, we were back home, and Mom and Dad and Timothy were all gibber-gabbering about which ski runs are their favorites and should Aldo take a morning lesson from a ski instructor and if it was supposed to snow or be sunny next weekend.

I stomped upstairs to my bedroom for some peace and quiet.

"Bogus," I said to my betta fish, "you're lucky. You get to stay in your cozy bowl, and you never have to go anywhere cold or snowy or outside your comfort zone."

I'D GIVE MY RIGHT GILL TO GET OUTSIDE THIS BOWL ZONE.

HANG 10*

I just woke up from one of those dreams where you surprise yourself at your own awesomeness.

I was in Hawaii with Jack and Bee and Mr. Mot. We were standing on a beach. The sand felt warm and soft on my bare toes, and the breeze smelled like a mixture of saltwater, tuna fish, and snowcones. My muscle-y left arm held up an orange-striped surfboard standing next to me.

Some pretty big waves were rolling in. "Let's catch one!" cried Mr. Mot. His surfboard was flowery colored. He had to kinda yell to be heard over the wooshy cacophony of the ocean.

"I'm in!" I yelled back.

"You are?" my real-life brain said to my dream-brain.

"Yuppers."

And with that I ran behind Mr. Mot and followed him into the water. We lay stomach-down on our surfboards and paddled out a ways. When the next big wave started rising, we stood up on the boards and rode the wave's wall down into its tube.

TUBE

WALL

LIP

WHITEWATER

"Look at you—balancing and moving at the same time," remarked Mr. Mot. Apparently my dream had pressed the mute button on the ocean's roar, so now we could chat while we surfed.

"Fer sure. I'm stoked." I gave him the *shaka* sign, which, to us surfers, means "hang loose.*"

HERE'S HOW: CURL UP ALL BUT YOUR PINKY AND THUMB, THEN WIGGLE YOUR HAND.

Surfing that wave was as easy as riding a moving sidewalk. All I had to do was stand there, bend my knees a little, and stick my arms out to the side. I waved at Jack and Bee, who gawked from the beach with their mouths agape. Then I bent over, planted the top of my noggin on the surfboard, and raised myself into a headstand— with no wall for balancing.

I rode the wave on my head all the way onto the shore then casually flipped upright. I was still completely dry except for my toes and fingers, since they'd been hanging over the edge of the board, into the water.

Aaannnd...then I got woken up by Timothy's halitosis.* His face was about 2 inches from mine, and his breath smelled like a mixture of saltwater, tuna fish, and snowcones. If the snowcones were barf flavor.

"Get up, bro," he said. "Time to go watch me get another hat-trick.*"

Ugh. Going to Timothy's hockey games is so boring, especially when it takes an hour to drive there, like today. At least I can work on my sketchbook during the car ride...and fondly remember my surfer day.

How much hotdogging would a hot dog do if a hot dog could hotdog?

HOTDOGGER

Hockey-wise, the best thing is the snacks.

Pretty much every ice-rink building has a little walk-up counter with a guy behind it selling soft pretzels, popcorn, candy, and stuff like that. Dad always slips me a few bucks between the first and second periods to go get whatever I want. I know it's basically a bribe so I won't whine about how Timothy's dumb hockey is taking up my whole Sunday, but I <u>like</u> bribes. I mean, I'm stuck there anyways. I might as well be stuck there with a snack in my mouth.

Today I picked a Slushie and a hot dog and brought them back to my cold, hard seat in the watcher-stands.

When you're looking down from the stands, you can tell which player is Timothy by the big number 17 on the back of his shirt. And also by his hyperspeed.* If you see a skater zooming in and out and around all the others like he's on fast-forward and everyone else is on regular, it's probably my brother. Have I mentioned he's a super-jock who likes to show off?

Hockey 101

Hockey is played on a giant, uber-slippery oval of ice. There's a goal with a net at each end. Each team has 6 players on the ice—5 regular players plus 1 kid that protects the goal, called the goalie. The players wear skates and carry long L-shaped sticks, which they use to hit a black puck and each other.

The game is divided into 3 chunks called "periods." The team with the most goals at the end of the 3rd period wins.

It's like soccer on ice, only faster and with shoving and the fans have to sit in a giant refrigerator to watch.

Yay hockey.

Just then, like he could read my mind, Timothy got tricksy. He was skating with the puck, and he got around the other team's guy who was in his way by spinning completely around, like a top on ice skates. The fans cheered and whistled. Then he passed the puck to himself by bouncing it off the blade of his skate and back to his stick. The fans stood up and hollered.* By now he was headed straight for the goal, and only one of the other team's skaters blocked his way. So he flipped the puck over the head of that guy, reached around, and with his stick, snagged the puck in mid-air and flicked it past the goalie. The fans went hysterical.*

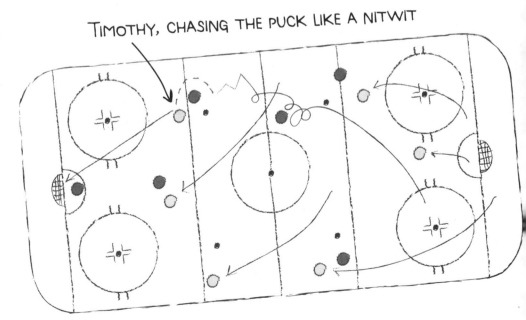

TIMOTHY, CHASING THE PUCK LIKE A NITWIT

After the hubbub* calmed down and Mom and Dad finally stopped high-fiving* everyone around them, Dad turned to me and said, "That brother of yours is quite the hotdogger!*"

I looked at the hot dog in my hand then back at my dad. He chortled.

"Actually, being a hotdogger has nothing to do with hot dogs," he said. "It means you're good at something athletic and you like to try risky or complicated moves to show it off."

"Oh. So Timothy's picture is probably in the dictionary next to the word hotdogger."

"Could be. And your picture is probably next to hotdogophile."

"That's not a word," I said, but he didn't hear me because he was on his feet again,

HOTDOGOPHILE

yelling along with everyone else. My hotdogger brother had scored his <u>third</u> goal of the game. A hat-trick—just like he promised.

On the drive home we stopped for Chinese. While Timothy and Mom and Dad relived every single second of the hockey game, I colored the dragon on my placemat. (Because until middle school I can still color sometimes, too, even in public, if I have nothing else to do and nobody else from Dana Elementary is there.)

CHOP SUEY PALACE

DINE IN • CARRY OUT
OPEN ON CHRISTMAS!

Then Timothy dared me to eat one of the red peppers out of his *kung pao* chicken.

Something I'm good at! I immediately thought, and I plucked up <u>3</u> of his peppers and popped them into my mouth.

Unfortunately, hotdogging hot peppers soon had me thrashing on the floor in pain. I was freaking out so much that my mom grabbed my hand and rushed me into the <u>ladies</u>' room (!), where she proceeded to stick my head under the faucet and scrub off my tongue with a wet paper towel. Ewww. But I let her because...well, I was dying.

Never, <u>ever</u> eat 3 hot peppers in 1 mouthful, even on a dare.

After we got home and I'd recovered, Mom brought me a fortune cookie, which she'd saved for me from Chop Suey. The fortune said:

ACT WITH CONFIDENCE, NO MATTER WHAT.

I dunno... Acting with confidence today nearly scorched to death one of my most prized possessions—my taste buds. But when Timothy acts with confidence, everyone leaps to their feet and cheers. What's up with that?

AT <u>LEAST</u> 1 BILLION, 314 MILLION POUNDS

Today Mr. Krug got back to Hercules.

He told us that Hercules' 4th chore was to catch a pig. No big deal. But the 5th thing he had to do was extremely gross: shovel the manure of 1,000 cows, goats, sheep, and horses.

And these weren't just regular old farm animals...they were immortal and for some reason pooped A LOT. And the barn they lived in hadn't been cleaned out for <u>30 years</u>.

The way I figure it, the math looks something like this:

1 REGULAR COW X 1 DAY =
120 POUNDS OF POOP
(I LOOKED IT UP.)
... TIMES 365 DAYS IN <u>1</u> YEAR...

So...

120 pounds x immortal poop factor x 1,000 farm animals x 365 days x 30 years = <u>Hideousness!!!</u>*

A king called Augeas owned the animals, and he said that Hercules had to clean out this potty barn in 1 <u>day</u>. Well, for a super-jock, Hercules was no dummy. He figured out pretty fast that if he <u>shoveled</u> all that manure, it would take his whole life. So instead, he dug ditches over to the barn from 2 rivers that happened to be close by. When the ditches were done, the rivers joined together, ran through the barn, and washed away the poo mountain.

"Now that's what I call gettin' 'er '<u>dung</u>,'" said Mr. Krug.

"Poop-scooping isn't exactly heroic,*" I said.

"This particular labor was designed to humiliate Hercules," said Mr. Krug. "Did it work?"

Jack raised his hand. "Not really, cuz he thought of it as a challenge. Plus, he was smart about it."

Huh. I guess that's true. And actually, it was probably more interesting than chasing a pig. Quite a bit horribler, but more interesting.

p.s. Today was so humdrum that on the walk home from school, Jack talked about this certain kind of rock called hematite,* and I listened to him.

DOOT-N-DOO-DOO

After homework tonight, Dad presented his famous chocolate-hazelnut layer cake and asked me if I wanted a slice.

I dropped my chin and raised one eyebrow at him. It's a look that means, *Are you even kidding me? Of course I want some.* (Try it. The look, I mean.)

A hockey game click-clacked on the TV while Timothy and I and Mom and Dad gathered around the table for dessert.

"Just 4 more days till our ski weekend, sport," said Dad. As he chewed, cake crumbs danced in his moustache.

"Ugh. Don't remind me."

"Why are you so against skiing, Aldo?" said Mom. She poured me a glass of milk, so that I would be getting some nutrition with my sugar.

"Because I always fall down! Last time we went, I spent most of the day lying <u>ON</u> the mountain instead of skiing <u>DOWN</u> the mountain."

THE BIGGER THEY ARE, THE HARDER THEY FALL.

ZIP IT, HALF-PINT!* IF I WEREN'T STUCK IN THIS HEAD-PLANT,* I'D... DO SOMETHING!

"I don't understand why you're such such a <u>wimp!</u>" said Timothy.

"No name calling," warned Dad.

"I'm <u>not</u> a wimp! It's just..." I sat up straight and put on my grown-up face. "I honor my unique specialness, which does not include skiing...and that's OK."

My Unique Specialness

FOOD SPANISH
TRUMPET SLIP-ONS
BACON FRIDAYS
FLEXIBILITY DOGS
SLUSHIES D&D
MEAT

Other People's Unique Specialness

SKIING SHOELACES
SPORTS MONDAYS
BEES NON-POTATO VEGETABLES
TOOTSIE ROLLS CATS

This was so hilarious to Timothy that milk leaked from his nose. Mom made him go take a shower. After he'd left the table, she said, "It's true that no one's good at everything, including your brother. But the last time we went skiing, you were only 8. Now you're almost 11! I think 8 is too young to decide that you can't do something."

"Yes!" cried Dad. "What if Milton Hershey* had decided at age 8 that his unique specialness didn't include chocolate!" He hoisted* a forkful of chocolate cake at me. "What if Sir Edmund Hillary* had one bad experience with heights as a child and never got up the gumption to climb again?" He stepped onto his chair and planted the forkful of cake in his mouth. "What if 8-year-old George Harrison* had taken his first guitar lesson, said 'Nah. This is too hard,' and became a haberdasher* instead?"

Then he jumped down from the chair, grabbed his guitar from its stand in the corner, and started playing that doot-n-doo-doo Beatles song, "Here Comes the Sun."

When he finally stopped with the singing, I said, "So you're saying I could be a gold-medal downhill skier someday? Because that seems pretty far-fetched..."

"Aldo, you're going to ski on the bunny hill this weekend," said Mom. "And you'll ride on the magic carpet lift, which never leaves the ground. Then if you're having fun and are feeling more confident, maybe you'll try the chairlift and one of the easy green runs with us. But only if you want to. OK?"

Both Mom and Dad were looking at me with their most encouraging "it's all right" smiles.

"OK, OK, OK. I'll <u>try</u>."

Blerg.

p.s. Other than the chocolate cake, today was so humdrum that I struck up a conversation with an icicle hanging outside my bedroom window. "Go away," I said. "I'm tired of you." His only reply? Icy silence. "Then you've left me no choice," I said. And I reached out my window and snapped him off. He tasted like frozen boringness.

HOOPIN' & HOLLERIN'

"We're going to Goosy's house," said Bee after school today. She was standing by the bent stop sign, waiting to highjack* me and Jack on our walk home.

"What for?" Jack said.

"Is snack included?" I said.

"You'll see," Bee said.

Girl secrets make me nervous. And usually I wouldn't go along with some harebrained* plan to visit my grandma right after school—even though my grandma's pretty cool—because I'm a kid of habit, and my after-school habit is to go straight home and watch TV. But I guess January's humdrummery makes even harebrained plans sound half-enticing. So off we went.

We found Goosy in her front yard. She was fussing with the face of a funny-looking snowman.

"Well if it isn't my favorite 5th graders!" she said, and she scooped us all into a group hug. "What do you think of my snow sculpture? I'm having a hard time finding the right pine needles for his moustache. Does it look like him?"

Fortunately, Goosy had a pitcher of horchata* waiting for us in her kitchen. While we sipped, she turned on the TV in her living room to a music video of a girl twirling one of those big plastic circle dealies around her stomach.

"Yay! I love hula hooping!" said Bee.

"Nobody can actually <u>do</u> that," I said.

"<u>We're</u> going to...right now!" said Goosy. And she got out a whole herd of hula hoops.

Just like snowpants shopping, this was a trap. I'd been hornswoggled* again!

"Nah. I'm good," I said. (I've started using "Nah, I'm good" because I've noticed that people accept it better than when I throw a fit or say "I don't want to" or "You're as crazy as a vegetarian hamburger if you think I'm doing that.") I set my hoop on the floor and criss-cross applesauced inside it.

THANKS, BUT I PREFER TO PRETEND THIS ISN'T HAPPENING.

"Aldo, you were the one grousing about how boring January is," said Bee. She was already wiggling her hula hoop in perfect circles, just like the girl in the video.

"Maybe you have to be thicker," said Jack as his hoop clattered to the floor.

"It's all in the hips, boys!" said Goosy. "Don't swing them in a circle...just put one foot in front of the other and rock your hips back and forth. There ya go, Jack! Nice! C'mon, Aldo! Give it a go!"

I'm pretty sure boys don't even <u>have</u> hips. That's what I wanted to <u>say,</u> but I <u>thought</u> it instead because I knew better than to start a conversation with my grandmother about boy butts versus girl butts. So I just watched and pressed my lips into a polite smile. I hoped this would all be over soon and I could go home to watch the History Channel. (Best. Shows. Ever.)

But as I watched, I noticed that the hula-hoop girl in the video spun the hoop around her neck sometimes and her arm sometimes and her leg sometimes, not just her stomach. And the song in the video had a catchy beat. And Jack and Bee and Goosy were all giggle-happy. And the cinnamony *horchata* was making my insides feel kinda, well, glad to be there.

I stood and put the hoop around my left arm, then I held that arm out to the side and moved my hand in a circle. And holy hamburgers, the hoop started to turn! The faster I circled my arm, the

faster the hula hoop hooped. Next I tried it around my belly. That was way harder, but once I got the hang of it,* *ba-zing*: I, Aldo Zelnick, was balancing myself <u>and</u> a hula hoop—and moving at the same time.

Bee noticed and gave me a "whoa, look at you!" face. I shrugged at her. I can't help it that I'm so clutch sometimes.

When we were all hooped out and it was time to go, Goosy said to me, "I'll see you Saturday for the ski trip!"

"You're skiing too?"

"Of course! Well, I might actually try snowboarding this time. It's never good to get too comfortable with your routines." And she winked at me and swatted my butt out the door.

Sigh. It's a hardship* having a grandma who's way brazener than you are.

p.s. After we left Goosy's, Jack asked me if I wanted to come with him to his mom-house for dinner. So I texted my dad, and he said I could. Mrs. Lopez is such a great cook that she should definitely have her own food show. She made us heavenly *huevos rancheros,** but all Jack ate was two scrambled *huevos* with white toast and strawberry jam, because he's just starting to add red foods to his all-beige diet.

p.p.s. Just because there were hula hoops and *huevos rancheros,* don't think that today wasn't humdrum. It was still January, and it still got dark before dinner. But come to think of it, that *horchata* did spice things up, just a little...

EVERYBODY'S GOIN' SURFIN' (WELL, JUST ME)

Mr. Mot and his guitar came over to our house tonight after dinner for the usual Wednesday-night jam session with my dad. But this time he also brought a Hawaii video and a real live surfboard!

He pulled the pointy fin parts off the bottom of the board so he could lay it down flat on the carpet in front of our TV. It was <u>way</u> longer and wider than an ironing board.

"I thought perhaps that catching some waves might ease your January doldrums," he said. "Take off your socks, my good man, and climb aboard!"

So I stepped onto the surfboard. It felt sturdy, like a piece of gym floor at Dana Elementary.

"Stand sideways. Put one foot back here, on the tail, and your other foot in the middle of the board," instructed Mr. Mot in his teachery voice. "Now crouch down a little. You want to keep your center of gravity low." Then he Velcroed a strap around my right ankle.

"Um, are you locking me to the surfboard?"

"This is called a 'leash.' It connects you to the board with a length of plastic rope. Hence,* when you wipe out, your surfboard won't get lost at sea. Also, I made this DVD for you. It's a compilation of YouTube videos of people—young people, mostly—surfing in Hawaii." Then he popped the disc into our DVD player...and I was surfing!

All the videos played teenager music in the background, and the people surfboarding were tan and smiley. It was like you were right there swooshing through the blue water with them. Even though my board stayed still, I bent and balanced and pretend-turned just like they did. I rode about 100 waves and was really getting the hang of it! Then, just when one muscle-y dude and I were about to hotdog a monster cruncher, I heard...

"*Hahahahaha.* You're too much of a wimp to <u>actually</u> surf."

Guess who.

"Oh yeah? Welp, too bad for you, 'cause <u>I'm</u> the one Mr. Mot's taking to Hawaii with him over spring break."

That part was pure hogwash,* but I thought Timothy might buy it—for a minute or 2 anyways. He did.

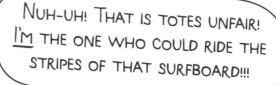

NUH-UH! THAT IS TOTES UNFAIR! <u>I'M</u> THE ONE WHO COULD RIDE THE STRIPES OF THAT SURFBOARD!!!

"And also," I added for an extra sprinkle of big-brother harassment,* "I have decided that I am going to get so good at skiing this weekend that by the end of the first day, <u>I'll</u> be beating <u>you</u> down the hill! In fact, I <u>dare you</u> to a race."

"Pffft. That's a joke." His words said *You're more full of poop than that barn in Hercules,* but his face said *Holy hat-trick. How'd my wimpy brother get so confident all of a sudden?*

"Ah, hubris*...," said Mr. Mot, who was passing by us on his way out the door. "Goodnight boys. Aldo, I'll come back for the surfboard tomorrow. Until then, you may continue your Hawaiian hotdogging."

Maybe Mr. Mot really <u>will</u> take me to Hawaii with him someday. Wouldn't that be awesome? If Timothy's extra nice to me, maybe I'll send him a postcard.

DEAREST BROTHER,

TODAY I WON FIRST PLACE IN THE VANS WORLD CUP SURFING CONTEST. THE PRIZE WAS $50,000.

WHEN I GET HOME, I WILL BUY YOU... A PACK OF GUM. SAY HELLO TO THE BELOW-ZERO WEATHER FOR ME.

Aldo Zelnick

TIMOTHY ZELNICK (FORMER ZELNICK FAMILY SUPER-JOCK)

c/o LOOSY GOOSY FORT COLLINS, CO

ALOHA

p.s. Today was so humdrum that I pretend-surfed in my living room and thought it was fun.

p.p.s. I looked up the word hubris tonight and wrote the meaning in the Word Gallery.

So is Mr. Mot saying that I'm being too confident—or that Timothy's being too confident—about our ski race? It must be the 2nd one.

BACON BOY IN THAT'S NOT A SURFBOARD FIN

TAKING A MID-WINTER VACATION TO HAWAII WAS A GREAT IDEA, BACON BOY.

I AGREE! ALL THAT JANUARY SNOW AND ICE...BRRR.

YEAH, PLUS THE SURFERS HERE NEED MY SKILLS. GOTTA GO TEACH THEM A FEW NEW TRICKS.

ALSO, T, WHERE'S YOUR SUNSCREEN? YOU'RE AS RED AS A TOMATO!

I CALL THIS ONE: THE BACON DOUBLE-CHEESEBURGER.

AND THIS ONE: THE LEFTOVER BACON. (NOTHING THERE. GET IT?)

AND THIS ONE: BRINGING HOME THE BACON.

WHAT HAPPENED TO HERCULES

Today Mr. Krug hurried through the rest of Hercules' 12 chores. Hercules had to:

6. Battle a bunch of man-eating birds.

7. Capture a bull.

8. Capture 4 man-eating horses. (Sheesh! What's with the carnivorous herbivores*?)

9. Steal a queen's belt.

10. Steal a giant monster's cows.

11. Steal some magic apples from some nymphs. (As far as I can tell, nymphs are just regular girls who like to dawdle around OUTSIDE.)

12. Capture a 3-headed dog, and he couldn't use any weapons. Oh, and the dog lives in the land of the dead people. Yikes.

HERCULES' JOB WOULD HAVE BEEN SO MUCH EASIER IF THAT DOG HAD BEEN HARMLESS* LIKE MAXIE-BOY!

"So what did we learn from Hercules and his labors?" asked Mr. Krug at the end. He sat down on his stool and used his handkerchief* to pat the sweat off his bald spot.

CAN I JUST SAY THAT HEAD-SWEAT GIVES ME THE HEEBIE-JEEBIES TOO?

"That if you do something bad you have to make up for it," said a kid in my class called Marvin Shoemaker.

"That sometimes you can win because you're stronger, but <u>sometimes</u> you can beat somebody even stronger than you by being smarter," said a different kid named Henry.

THAT ANCIENT GREECE WAS CHOCK-FULL OF BIZARRE CREATURES.

AND CRIMINAL BEHAVIOR.

"That you have to keep trying," said Jack.

"So what happened to Hercules after he finished all his labors?" asked Henry.

"Good question," said Mr. Krug. "Hercules had hundreds more adventures. He joined the Argonauts in search of the Golden Fleece. He fell in love, he rescued Prometheus, he attacked Troy. He kept on being a hero until the day he died."

Geez. I guess if Hercules can have <u>hundreds</u> of adventures, I could have a couple...

p.s. On the humdrum scale, with 10 being as boring as having to sit quietly at a fancy restaurant for an hour after you're done eating so your parents can "enjoy their meals"...or wait, make that as boring as the worst teacher you've ever had talking and talking and talking at you about something like the history of trade routes in Holland, I'd give today a 5. I don't know why. I guess I'm just in a more hopeful* mood.

BORN TO HANDBALL

LET'S ROLL.

HOW COME NOBODY TOLD US ABOUT THE SPHERE THING?

THEY TOLD ME. I JUST PREFER TO BE HORIZONTAL.*

Timothy's bedroom is like a ball store. Any kind of ball you want, there's probably at least one on his dresser or in his closet or under his bed.

So this morning before school, I ambled into his room and said, "Yo. I need a ball."

"Get outta here," he growled. "Wait... <u>You</u> want a <u>ball</u>?"

"Yeah," I shrugged. "I was thinking it'd be good to show the other kids a new game at recess. You know—keep everybody on their toes. What would you recommend?"

When Timothy's dumbstruck, he looks an awful lot like Bogus.

"Uhhh...," he finally said. "Me and my friends at Dana Elementary used to play handball against the big brick wall..." He got down on

his stomach to reach under his bed. He scooped out an assortment of balls and about 37 smelly socks. He handed me a blue rubber ball. It was bigger than a hacky sack but smaller than a baseball.

"It smells like feet," I said.

"That's my signature fragrance," Timothy said as he waved me out into the hallway to show me how handball works. "You start by throwing the ball against the wall. It will bounce back and hit the ground. After it bounces up from the ground—and it can only bounce once—the person who's closest to it has to hit it against the wall again. If that person misses, he's out. The last person left wins."

He tossed the blue ball at our hall wall. It came towards me. I swung at it with my left fist, and it hit the stair railing, bounced down the stairs, and plonked my mom, who was carrying up a basket of laundry, in the forehead.

"Nice to see you boys playing together," she said. Since Timothy's been a super-jock from the day he was born, she's used to getting clobbered by flying sporting goods.

"Aldo, don't hit it with your <u>fist</u>," said Timothy. "Use your open hand. Geez, do I have to tell you everything?"

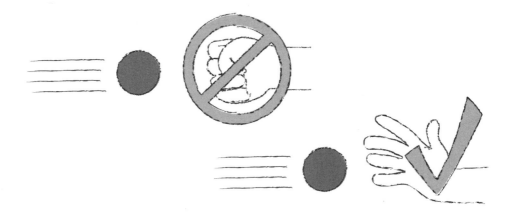

Then he made me go outside and play handball with him against the garage door until I could hit the ball "without looking like a spaz" is how he put it. He even taught me a couple hotdogger moves.

So when lunch recess came around today, I led Jack and Bee and Danny and a few other hangers-on* over to the big brick wall and pulled the blue ball from my pocket.

"Lemme show ya how it's done," I said, and I proceeded to teach the gang how to handball.

"You're awesome, Aldo!" said Bee after we'd played for a while and I'd nailed a perfect headsie.*

"Yeah, I think my hotdogger genes are finally kicking in," I said. "Not like it's a big deal or anything."

On the walk home from school, I stopped at Jack's dad-house with Jack because he wanted to show me his new hematite rocks. What can I say. That's just how good of a friend I am.

So there we were, admiring a handful of lovely black pebbles. Jack's dad (his name is Fritz; he's a fireman) was making us after-school peanut butter sandwiches.

"I hear your family's going skiing this weekend," said Fritz. "Sounds fun."

I POLISHED THEM MYSELF IN MY ROCK TUMBLER!

THEY LOOK LIKE BLACK JELLY BEANS. IS THIS A HOAX*? I'D BETTER TASTE ONE...

"Yeah, I think it'll be fun," I agreed. "At first I didn't want to go... but lately I decided I'm good at skiing." (I was practicing my confidence.)

He raised his eyebrows, frowned his mouth, and bobbed his head. "I bet you <u>are</u>. Actually, I was thinking maybe Jack and I could ski <u>with</u> you. He's never been before. You could show him how."

About then, Jack choked a little on his peanut butter. He's not growing into his athletic abilities yet like I am into mine.

"Sure!" I said. "And you guys would stay in the same condo as us?"

"Maybe in the condo next door," said Fritz. "So you and Jack could be ski bums together, but there would be plenty of beds to sleep everyone. Whatcha say, boys?"

ANOTHER P.B.O., JACK-ATTACK?

SKIING REQUIRES LOTS OF ENERGY!

"Sweet! I've never been on vacation with my best friend before." I put my arm around Jack's shoulder and squeezed. Then I looked at his face. I recognized that face. It was the face I had on when Timothy first told me about the ski trip.

"Don't worry," I whispered. "It's easy. All you have to do is try." Being brave is easier, I've noticed, if you're doing it to help someone else.

EQUIPPED FOR SUCCESS

It's Friday morning. Just one more day of school, then it's the start of our ski weekend! Are you as excited as I am? Be back later.

After school today, my dad and Jack's dad took me and Jack to rent ski equipment.

"See, skiing is a whole big hoopla,*" I explained to Jack in the car on the way to the rental place. "The first thing you do is try on ski boots and walk around in them. They're not like regular boots at all. They feel like you're walking around in buckets of cement, but you get used to it. Then they clamp you into the skis. That part doesn't feel weird. Not until the skis are pointed downhill, on top of slippery snow."

"Is it like skateboarding down a big hill?" asked Jack. His face looked kinda pale, even though his skin is usually way browner than mine is. "Because I can only skateboard on flat streets."

"Not really... Well, yeah, maybe if you had two really <u>long</u> skateboards and your feet were glued onto them. Here, have a sip of my Coke. I think you need some sugar or something."

At the ski shop, the people got us all set up. Besides warm clothes and snacks, you need special equipment to go downhill skiing. Here's a diagram.

Jack and I rented everything except the goggles. You have to buy those. My dad and the rest of my family and Fritz already have their own ski equipment, so they didn't get anything.

On the drive back to our neighborhood, Dad and Fritz swapped ski stories in the front seat while Jack and I played Slug Bug in the back seat. Jack saw 3 Bug cars, and I only saw 1. That's OK. I was the one who said we should play, but I only suggested it so that Jack wouldn't notice my dad's story about the time he accidentally went off a ski jump and broke his leg. Ouch.

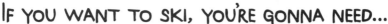

IF YOU WANT TO SKI, YOU'RE GONNA NEED...

TWO SKIS THAT ARE ABOUT AS TALL AS YOU ARE. THESE LITTLE FOOT-HOLDERS ARE CALLED **BINDINGS**.

A HELMET TO PROTECT YOUR BRAIN IN CASE YOU CRASH.

GOGGLES. THEY'RE LIKE SCUBA GOGGLES, ONLY WITH DARK LENSES AND NO NOSE-AND-MOUTHPIECE.

A PAIR OF BOOTS THAT ARE SUPPOSED TO CLAMP TIGHT AROUND YOUR FEET AND LEG BOTTOMS. (THE SKI SHOP GUY SAID JACK MIGHT NEED EXTRA SOCKS.)

TWO POLES—ONE FOR EACH HAND. THE POLES ARE ABOUT AS LONG AS YOUR LEGS.

A GOOD, CAN-DO ATTITUDE. PROBABLY YOUR <u>MOST</u> IMPORTANT ITEM.

"Wanna hack?" I asked Jack when we got to my house. Weirdly, I was in high spirits.*
"Timothy will play too."

So the 3 of us hacky sacked until dinnertime and Jack and his dad went home. And whaddya know... I actually kicked the ball a few times.

p.s. Tonight, after hoagies* for dinner, we watched *The Hobbit*. The *Lord of the Rings* movies are pretty lonnng, but this one wasn't humdrum at all. It was a little sad, though—especially the part in the beginning when all the dwarves show up at Bilbo's house and eat every last bit of <u>his</u> delicious hobbit food!

I have to go to bed now because <u>tomorrow</u> we're driving to Steamboat Springs. It's a ski town about 2 movies away. 'Night.

TSK, TSK. THESE CRUMBS WERE ALL THOSE DWARVES LEFT BEHIND... WHAT. HAVE YOU NEVER SEEN A HOBBIT HAMSTER BEFORE?

UP AND OVER

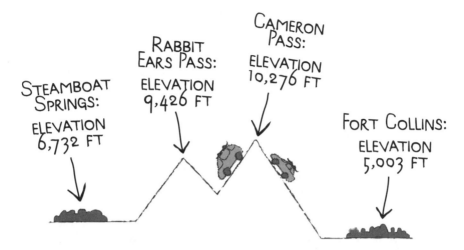

CAMERON PASS:
ELEVATION 10,276 FT

RABBIT EARS PASS:
ELEVATION 9,426 FT

STEAMBOAT SPRINGS:
ELEVATION 6,732 FT

FORT COLLINS:
ELEVATION 5,003 FT

I'm sitting in the car on the way to Steamboat, or "The Boat," as ski aficionados like me call it for short.

I'm in our minivan with Mom, Dad, Goosy, Timothy, and Max. Jack and his dad are behind us in their car. I already watched 1 movie on Mom's laptop, but now I'm bored with that, so I'm putting in some sketchbook time instead of putting in another movie.

This skinny road from my house to Steamboat squiggles up, up, up. If you're a kid who gets car sick, definitely bring a barf bag. And gum. As we get higher and higher, my ears keep doing that thing where they close up and I can't hear anymore, so I have to keep chewing to unplug them. (Though plugged-up ears are handy* if your dad and your grandma are singing "Winter Wonderland," like mine are right now.)

Next to the road are steep, mountainy hills made of rock. Hey! That must be why they call them the Rocky Mountains! But I guess there's dirt on top of a lot of the rock, because billions of pine trees grow all over the mountains too. And cuz it's January, the rocks and hills and trees are thick-frosted with snow.

Which reminds me, for breakfast this morning, before we left our house, Dad made "ski mountain pancakes." Each of us got our own stack of pancakes dusted in powdered sugar with a whipped-cream peak on top. Little people made from honeydew* melon skied down the mountain on bacon-strip skis.

WHO NEEDS THE BREAKFAST OF CHAMPIONS, WHEN YOU'VE GOT THE CHAMPION OF BREAKFASTS?

"I have a good feeling about this ski trip, sport," Dad said with a wink as he handed me my edible mountain.

"Me too!"

"I have a feeling I'm gonna kick some Aldo booty," said Timothy.

"You should be encouraging your little brother, not teasing him," scolded Mom.

"It's OK," I said. "I challenged him to a race. You gotta act with confidence no matter what, right?"

"Someone's feeling audacious!" said Goosy. She high-tenned* me from across the breakfast table. Goosy loves audaciousness.

She also loves me drawing in this sketchbook. I just looked over at her now, in the minivan chair next to me. She has her sketchbook out for the car trip too. Weird. It looks like she's drawing a stripey fish... OK, I just asked Goosy what she's sketching. She said it's a certain kind of fish that she and Mr. Mot were talking about yesterday.

Here. I copied Goosy's fish (and added some of my own details) so you can see what it looks like.

I'M THE STATE FISH OF HAWAII.

OH YEAH? WELL...I'M THE STATE FISH OF ALDO'S ROOM.

Goosy spelled the fish's name for me too. It's uber long. Are you ready?

Humuhumunukunukuapua'a*

"Why were you and Mr. Mot talking about Hawaii fish, anyways?" I asked her.

"Because he's on a Hawaii kick lately for some reason. Whenever I see him these days, it's Hawaii this and Hawaii that. He's hog-wild* for the place!"

"Yeah," I sighed. "Hawaii looks pretty great. I want to go surfing! But here we are, in Colorado, in January, so...I guess I'll surf the ski slopes instead."

"Such a wise grandson I have," she said. Then to my dad she said, "Leo, let's pull over up there to stretch our legs and take in some of this Rocky Mountain grandeur."

And that's what we did:

CONDOHHH!

We're at the condo! We're at the condo!

In case you don't know, condo is short for condominium, which is basically an apartment-house you can rent if you go somewhere vacationy...

...Like Hawaii, which is where Mr. Mot's brother's condo is, remember? And where I will stay when Mr. Mot brings me there someday.

We carried in our clothes bags and ski equipment and food. Jack and his dad took their stuff into their condo, which is attached right next to ours like a Lego. Then Jack and Max and I walked all through both condos to see whose was better. They were pretty much the same, except Jack's has a black bear rug nailed to one wall, and mine has a second TV, in the loft.

"Yours is better," said Jack.

"Yup."

THIS IS WHAT THE CONDO LOOKS LIKE WHEN I'M SITTING ON THE LIVING ROOM COUCH AND I'M LOOKING UP AT THE LOFT.

On our walk-about, Jack and I also peeked in all the closets and drawers. We found a bunch of weird stuff, like long underwear, a harmonica, a drawerful of board games, a hairbrush with hair stuck in it (ew), a picture of someone's dog, a baby's high chair, some toy handcuffs, and, hanging in one closet, a hole-y sweater.

99

We walked by Mom. "Where'd you get that?" she asked me.

I had to stop playing the harmonica to answer her. "Under a bed."

"Well, when you're done with it, put it back where you found it, OK?"

Have you ever noticed that parents are big on putting things back where you found them, even when it makes no sense?

A little later, while the grown-ups made dinner, Timothy hooked up our Xbox to the TV in the loft, so us kids would have something to do until spaghetti. Then after we ate, we all put on our swimsuits—with pants and shirts and coats on top of them...because it's January outside! And we got in our cars and drove a few minutes away, to the Steamboat hot springs.*

I'M READY! WOULD YOU HAVE GUESSED THERE'S A BEACH BODY UNDER ALL THIS?

Get this: Hot springs are like giant hot tubs the earth makes for you. Apparently hot water just comes shooting out of the ground in certain places, so if you build a swimming pool where one of these natural hot-water faucets is, *bam*—you've got yourself a toasty-warm pool for swimming outdoors even in the middle of a Colorado winter. (And <u>now</u> I get why this town is called Steamboat <u>Springs</u>.)

So there we were at the hot springs, chillaxing in water so warm it was like taking a bath, even though the lifeguards, who were standing on the ground next to the pool, were shivering in their puffy winter coats. Steam rose all around us. And then it started to snow! It reminded me of my dad sifting powdered sugar on top of our pancake mountains—only this was like the big man upstairs was sifting snowflakes over the actual mountains.

Which is when Timothy interrupted. He'd been Spidermanning up and down the climbing wall at one edge of the hot pool, but next thing I knew, his seal-like head popped up in the water next to me. "Hey, Aldo!" he said. "I dare you to a race down the big slides!"

Yes, the hot springs center here also has twin giant slides that start up high in the air and corkscrew down into a pool next to the one we were in. In the dark the slides looked like death tunnels from a Batman movie you're not supposed to watch when you're 10.

"Pretty sure the slides aren't open at night," I said, relieved.

"Pretty sure they <u>are</u>, cuz I just asked that lifeguard."

Goosy leaped out of the pool and started walking to the slide entrance. "C'mon boys!" she yelled. "I'll judge who wins!"

Jack looked at me. Timothy looked at me. I looked at me. I mean, I sort of had this weird out-of-my-body split-second where I saw myself like I'd been trying to be lately, like one of those confident kids who doesn't hesitate,* who just <u>does</u> things. I must admit, I looked pretty good. Herculean, even.

So I hoisted myself out of the pool and hustled to the slides. Jack climbed the stairs to the top with Timothy and me to say "Go!", and Goosy waited in the water at the bottom to declare the winner.

That's right, you're reading the sketchbook of the winner of the first annual Zelnick Steamboat Hot Springs Slide Contest.

I'm not gonna lie...all 230 feet of that slide were cold and dark and fast and hair-raising.* But I did it, and now Timothy's a little apprehensive that I'll beat him in tomorrow's ski race too. I could tell by the look of total disbelief on his face as he watched Goosy carry me on her shoulders in a splashy victory march around the pool.

HIGH HOPES

Welp, today's the day I prove once and for all that I, Aldo Valentine Zelnick, am a doer. Sure, I have my own unique specialness, but that doesn't mean I don't at least <u>try</u> all different kinds of things. Even things where you have to move and balance at the same time.

I just woke up. It's still dark outside. Nobody else is awake yet. I brought my sketchbook into the bathroom so I could turn on the light and get focused for the big day ahead. Here goes.

I can <u>ski</u>.

I <u>can</u> ski.

<u>I</u> can ski.

Can I ski? Oh geez. What if I can't?

WHOOOA THERE, BIG FELLA. HOLD YOUR HORSES.* DON'T GET CAUGHT UP IN NEGATIVE THINKING. YOU CAN DO ANYTHING YOU PUT YOUR MIND TO.

LIKE, JUST LATELY YOU LEARNED TO HULA HOOP!

(OK, THAT'S MAYBE NOT SOMETHING TO TRUMPET, CUZ YOU DON'T REALLY WANNA BE KNOWN AS THE HULA HOOP KID, BUT STILL.)

YOU ALSO PICKED UP HACKY SACK (KINDA), AND YOU COULD PROBABLY GO PRO WITH HANDBALL. PLUS, YOU OWNED THAT GIANT SLIDE LAST NIGHT, RIGHT?

Thanks for the pep talk, Hercules. Now I'm gonna try a trick that Goosy always talks about. I'm gonna close my eyes and picture myself skiing like it's no big deal. Visualize what you want to happen and it will happen, she says. BRB.

Wow. I'm a better skier than I <u>thought</u>.

I shut my eyes and concentrated real hard. I saw myself at the top of the white, snow-covered hill. I pointed my skis toward the bottom then swished back and forth, back and forth, down the mountain like it was no big deal. Then I took the magic carpet ride back to the top and zig-zagged down a 2nd time.

Huh. That was fun. I'm gonna do that again.

Holy snowflakes, I'm getting really good at skiing now. This time I imagined challenging Timothy to that race I dared him about, and in the middle we ended up going off a jump and flying through the air for like 10 seconds. I was so naturally talented at ski jumping that once again Timothy was dumbstruck:

Annnd...then I beat him to the bottom of the hill. Yup, in my mind movie, I won the ski race. By a mile. Actually, I was such a hotshot* that right now, just sitting here on the toilet, I feel a little sorry for Timothy. He's still sleeping and doesn't even know how badly he's gonna get beaten today. Poor kid.

All that skiing made me hungry. I'm gonna go eat a Pop-tart or something for 1st breakfast, then I can have 2nd breakfast with everyone else after they wake up.

It's almost time to leave for the ski mountain now. I'm all dressed and ready to go. So is everyone else. We're just waiting for Jack to finish getting ready. He was kind of a hindrance* this morning.

Here's what happened: I ate my Pop-tart and played on Mom's laptop for a while, then finally everyone else started waking up. Fritz came over to our condo to help make hash browns and ham-and-cheese omelets. After most of us were done eating, he asked me to run next door to make sure Jack was awake and tell him to come to breakfast.

So I stepped inside the front door at Jack's condo and yelled, "Jack! Breakfast! We're gonna leave for skiing pretty soon!"

"I can't!" he said. I could see his face peeking through the loft railing down at me.

"Yes you can! Don't let negative thinking control your destiny! C'mon!"

"I mean I can't! I'm stuck!"

"What?" I ran up the stairs. There was Jack, on the floor, with one arm handcuffed to the railing.

"Hey! Those are the toy handcuffs we found!"

Jack looked heartbroken.* I thought he might even cry. Which mostly you don't do in front of your best friend, unless you break your arm or something really serious.

"I woke up in the middle of the night," he said in a rush, like water down that steep water slide. "And I was lying here thinking that skiing is scary and I don't want to go. And I had the handcuffs in my pocket cuz I was messing around with them when you were playing the harmonica, only I didn't put them back where I found them. And for some reason it seemed like a clutch idea to handcuff myself to the railing so I wouldn't have to ski. Ya know how stupid things seem smart when you're half-asleep? Then I musta fallen back asleep, and when I woke up, my dad wasn't here. So now I can't go skiing...but I also can't go to the bathroom. And I really have to go..." Jack made a gulpy noise and looked up at me with melty brown eyes.

"Don't worry, Jack," I said, stepping over to give the handcuffs a tug. (Dang they make those things strong. Even kid Hercules couldn't muscle them open.) "You are not going to wet your pajamas—not on my watch."

Be a doer, Aldo, I thought. OK, what would Hercules do? Cut off Jack's hand with a lightning bolt? Find the nymph who has the key? Go get help from a magical creature? Ack! Hercules, you are no help in real-life emergencies...wait!

"I know!" I said. "Your dad's a fireman. Firemen are helpful in real-life emergencies." And I ran back to my condo, grabbed Fritz, and took him to Jack. Sure enough, Fritz had some special fireman tools in his car, and in about a second, he'd snipped the toy handcuffs in half and Jack was free to...well, you know.

Whew.

OK, my dad just told me it's time to go skiing now for reals. Don't worry—Jack'll be fine today. Maybe on the ride to the ski area I'll teach him the hallucinate* Hercules trick that helped my confidence this morning. On second thought, writing that out loud makes me sound crazy. I think I'll keep my pretend chats with Hercules hush-hush.*

THE DAY ALDO
LEARNED TO SKI

Welp, it's Monday. President's Day. The second day of skiing for the weekend. Only we're not skiing. We're back home in Fort Collins, and I'm on the couch resting.

So what happened, you ask? More like what <u>didn't</u> happen.

When we got to the ski area, it looked like a postcard. The sky was Smurf blue, and the sun was acting like it was summer. And under the great big sky sat a tiny little mountain frosted in snow, with a few pine trees sprinkled on top.

"It's called Howelsen Hill," Mom said as we pulled up. "It's the oldest ski area in Colorado. And it's small, so we thought you'd feel comfortable here today, Aldo."

"I'm not sure if I should ski it or pet it," said Timothy.

"I'm gonna snowboard it!" said Goosy with a whoop, and with that, all of us clamped on our bucket-of-cement-feeling ski boots, picked up our skis and poles, and clomped our way from the parking lot to the ski building to get lift tickets.

"I'm already tired," I said to Jack.

"I'm already having cold feet," said Jack.

"But this place does look super easy."

"You think so?"

"Dude, we've <u>sledded</u> down hills bigger than this one."

"Yeah. I guess so."

Once we all had tickets hanging from the pull handles of our coat zippers, the dads took me and Jack to the bunny hill, while Mom, Timothy, and Goosy went off to do their thing.

HOWELSEN HILL SKI AREA

5th GRADER COMP TICKET

CHILD 1 DAY

A LIFT TICKET IS ACTUALLY A STICKER THAT YOU FOLD AND STICK TO ITSELF AROUND A WIRE THINGY CALLED A WICKET.

The magic carpet ride was just like Mom promised: You clamp on your skis, shuffle onto the lift (which really is just like a moving sidewalk), and let it carry you up the hill. Even Jack thought that part was easy-peasy.

ALL UPHILL HIKES SHOULD HAVE THESE. AM I RIGHT, OR AM I RIGHT?

Thennn...suddenly you're standing at the top of a slippery hill with slippery skis on your feet and you're thinking the bunny hill is not actually as cute and harmless as it sounds.

But my dad and Fritz made sure that Jack and I stood with our skis sideways across the mountain instead of pointing down the mountain while they explained to us what to do next.

"It's called the bunny hill because it's so little you can practically be down it in 1 hop," said Fritz. (He's basically Mr. Grown-Up Super-jock—like Timothy will be 30 years from now. Which is weird to think about.) "But <u>you're</u> not going to hop. You're going to pizza."

"Now you're talkin'!" I said.

It turned out that pizza is a ski word for how you position your skis. You see, if you point your skis straight down the mountain like French fries, you'll go fast. Jack and I didn't want to go fast. So to go slow, we had to make our skis into the shape of a piece of pizza, like this:

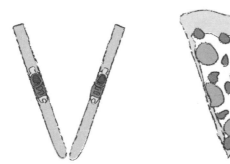

"Personally, I like French fries and pizza about the same," I said, "but pizza is definitely better for skiing."

With Fritz and my dad pizzaing alongside us, Jack and I skied all the way down to the bottom of the bunny hill. Without falling. Even once.

Jack grinned at me.

"Good job!" I said. I high-fived him, and he fell over.

So Jack and I magic carpeted up and pizzaed down the bunny hill a whole bunch of times, until I said, "OK, turns out skiing isn't scary. It's <u>boring</u>."

"Yeah," Jack agreed. "It's kinda boring."

"Time to teach you boys to turn!" said Fritz, and instead of pizzaing straight down the bunny hill again, he showed us how to pizza our skis but turn back and forth, like this: ⟶

Turning was harder than straight pizzaing, but it still wasn't that hard. About 10 more times down the bunny hill and Jack and I were turning masters.

"OK, this time I dare you to a race," I said to Jack as we got off the magic carpet.

"First one to the trash can," he said.

So we raced down to the bottom of the bunny hill and I won! And I never win speed races.

"Ready for lunch?" said Dad about then. "Your mom just texted me that she and Timothy and Goosy are waiting for us in the snack bar."

"There's a snack bar? Sweet!"

So all of us gathered for lunch and swapped stories about our ski morning. Timothy and Mom had already skied the entire mountain, including the blacks. In case you don't speak skiing like I do, here's how the ski run colors work:

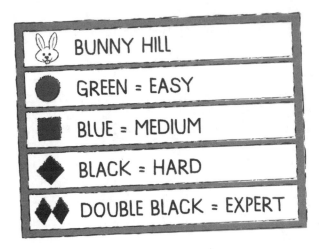

🐰	BUNNY HILL
●	GREEN = EASY
■	BLUE = MEDIUM
◆	BLACK = HARD
◆◆	DOUBLE BLACK = EXPERT

"I've been shredding the greens today," said Goosy. "They're hunky-dory.*"

"Are you boys ready for a green run?" Mom asked Jack and me.

I looked at Jack. He shrugged. "Sure...," he said. His face didn't look so sure.

"You'll need to take the chairlift...," she said.

"It's time to give the toddlers back their magic carpet lift, right Aldo?" said Timothy.

I stood and scowled at my hotdogger brother. Then I snapped my ski goggles over my eyes, turned to leave, and zinged him back with, "Haters gonna hate.* Let's ski, Jack." And with the Hercules in my head cheering me on, I led the way to the chairlift.

Which was scary, by the way. Not the being-up-in-the-air part, but the getting-on-and-off part. The chairs just keep moving, and you have to sit down at the right time to get on and stand up at the right time to get off. It's kinda like getting on and off one of those old-timey playground merry-go-rounds when it's already spinning, or hopping into a jump-rope that someone else is already turning.

It's tricky, and it takes a good sense of timing, which usually is not part of my unique specialness. But my dad helped me, and Jack's dad helped him, and next thing I knew we were standing at the top of the world.

But I didn't even hesitate. I just started
skiing. A little French fry, a little pizza, turning
back and forth, back and forth, all the way down
Howelsen Hill. And Jack stayed right behind me. I
guess it's easier to be a follower when you have a
brave hero leading the way.

Partway down the mountain I even stopped watching my skis (to make sure they were French frying when they were supposed to French fry and pizzaing when they were supposed to pizza). Instead, I looked up and noticed that the snow sparkled like Valentine glitter and the blue sky spread out all over us in a way that made me feel little and big at the same time.

My mom and dad and Fritz mostly stayed behind us, so I couldn't see them. Of course, Timothy showed off, racing past us and skiing in and out of the trees at the edge of the run. He even lay down in the snow a couple times, like the hare* in that lesson story where the turtle is slower than the rabbit but beats him anyway.

Goosy boarded downhill from me, making wild squiggles across the snow. I saw her wipe out a bunch of times, but as we French fried to the chairlift to ride it back up the mountain again, I realized that Jack and I had just skied a green run without head-planting <u>even</u> <u>once</u>.

"So you and I...we're skiers," I said to Jack on the ride up. Fritz sat between us and handed us each a mini candy bar, cuz that's one of the things you do when you're a skier—you fuel up on the chairlift.

"I know!" said Jack. "We're totally getting the hang of it! This time, let's see if we can <u>ski faster</u>."

We figured out that skiing faster meant French frying more than pizzaing and taking a straighter path down the mountain than a wide, back-and-forth one. It was pretty fun, and when I found myself speeding past a toddler in a helmet, I knew that this would go down in Zelnick history as "The Day Aldo Learned to Ski."

Oh sure, skiing faster also meant that Jack and I head-planted a few times, but it was no big deal. Our dads helped us back up, and we skied on.

Up and down and up and down the mountain we went. I was on the chairlift with my dad and Timothy when Dad said, "I think this'll be the last run of the day, boys. These old knees of mine would like to head back to the condo and soak in the hot tub."

"Ya know what that means, little bro," said Timothy. "It's race time."

THIS IS TIMOTHY'S RACE FACE. SCARY, HUH?

"Whoa, whoa, whoa," said Dad. "We've had a wonderful ski day together. Let's not write an unhappy ending."

But my inner Hercules wanted a win. "You're on!" I said to Timothy.

So at the top of a run called The Mile, Jack said, "Good luck!" and Goosy said, "Go!" Timothy gave me a 60-second head start, which I figured was only fair since he's 4 years older.

Zooom. I was French frying like a McDonald's drive-thru. I bent my knees deeper so I'd go faster. The air whipped my cheeks, and my skis vibrated like a Slushie machine. I tucked my poles up under my armpits and leaned forward. Now I know why Timothy likes hotdogging, I realized. It feels like the best parts of a video game only in real life.

But wait! Here came Timothy, beelining right by me! He swiveled his head back to me to flash his super-jock grin, and in that split-second he must have, by the grace of Hercules, caught a patch of ice, because his left ski shot out from under him and down he went, skis and poles shooting this way and that.

BIFF!

I steered around his yard sale (that's ski lingo for a crash where your gear ends up all over the mountain) and kept on going. Holy hotdogger, I was gonna win! Then I noticed a shortcut. If I made a quick right, I'd get to the bottom faster and beat Timothy for sure! As I rounded the corner onto the shortcut, I saw, out of the corner of my goggle, a sign with a black diamond.

◆ WORST IDEA EVER! →

Uh-oh.

But it was too late. I was suddenly on a really steep run for really good skiers, and there was nothing I could do about it but let gravity do what gravity does.

I'm pretty sure <u>my</u> yard sale was the most
spectacular one Howelsen Hill has ever held. As I
somersaulted like the rocks in Jack's rock tumbler,
skis and poles and goggles and gloves and chunks
of snow flew in all directions. And finally, when
everything came to a stop, there was only Fritz's
face right up next to mine and pain like a honker
wave dragging me under.

"Owww!" I yelled.

"Lie still, pal," said Fritz. "Where does it hurt?"

"My arm!"

Next thing I knew, the face of a girl with yellow hair was right next to Fritz's face. She was talking to me all gentle and nice.

"I'm dead, aren't I," I wailed between sobs. "I've heard you see angels when you're dying, but I never really believed it..."

"My name is Hazel. I'm ski patrol," she said. "I'm going to wrap this splint around your arm, then I'm going to strap you onto this sled and take you down the mountain. I know it hurts, but you're going to be fine."

HOW MANY FINGERS AM I HOLDING UP?

Yup, I broke my right arm. Hazel and Fritz took me to the hospital, where a doctor gave me some medicine to take away the pain but that also made me sleepy, and when I woke up, my mom was holding my hand on my un-demolished side, and the rest of my family was standing around my emergency-room bed, and my arm was mummied in a yellow cast. (I stuck a piece of the cast tape to the cover of the sketchbook for you to see. You might not have noticed, but it's a harbinger* of how this whole ski story turned out.)

A lot happened yesterday, and today I'm back home, couch-surfing and writing in my sketchbook. At least I'm left-handed.

Timothy just brought me a plate of Chinese take-out and a fortune cookie. He's been weirdly nice to me today. The fortune said:

DO NOT CONFUSE RECKLESSNESS WITH CONFIDENCE.

Oh sure. <u>Now</u> it tells me.

APRÈS-SKI

If there's a silver lining to having a broken arm, it's that it skyrockets your popularity. At school today all the kids wanted to sign my cast and hear the story of what happened.

"Yeah, I headed down a black diamond," I told them at recess. "I musta caught an edge or something because I took a pretty hard spill. Had to go to the hospital and everything, but it wasn't that big of a deal. I'm just sorry I'm gonna miss out on skiing <u>next</u> weekend..."

Bee wasn't buying it though. "Jack said you took a wrong turn," she mentioned after the rest of the kids got busy handballing.

"Well, I <u>probably</u> should have stayed on the green run, but Timothy and I were racing, and I was hotodoggin' it pretty thoroughly..."

"Yeah, he also told me you're a good skier. I'm proud of you, Aldo. I know you were anxious about skiing, but you did it!"

"*Pffft.* Skiing's not that hard. It's the <u>ground</u> that's hard, when you bounce down it at a hundred miles an hour, anyways. Don't let snow fool you—it's <u>not</u> the soft and fluffy bunny of precipitation it pretends to be."

And then Bee joined the handballers, and I just had to stand there and watch. Funny...standing and watching used to be part of my unique specialness, but today it didn't feel so special. It just felt ho-hum.* And lonely.

BACON BOY:
BIG BACONS DON'T CRY

It's Friday after school already. I haven't picked up this sketchbook for a few days because, well, I've been feeling kinda heavy-hearted.*

Which was the perfect emotion for a weird type of poem that Mr. Krug taught us about in Language Arts today. They're called *haikus,* and they're these 3-liners that like to be sorta naturey or depressing and don't even rhyme.

You get 17 syllables total, and you have to break them up like this:

> 5 syllables first
> Next comes 7 syllables
> Then 5 syllables

(That was a haiku right there! Did you notice?)

So for example:

Skiing the mountain
Brave and fast like Hercules
Ends in a yard sale

Or:

Time for vacation
Sandy beach or snowy hill?
Hawaii, of course

Or:

Month of dark and ice
Every day, humdrummery
January blahs

Or:

Hotdogging takes skill
But hanging back is safer
Broken arm and dreams

Welp, that about sums it up. Jack's coming over in a few minutes, and we're gonna watch a movie or something. *Sigh.* I can hardly even work a video game controller with this dumb cast.

CHEESE PIZZA
+   PINEAPPLE
+   HAM
_____
= HAWAIIAN PIZZA!

HULA PARTY

Jack came over all right. And so did Bee and Danny and Goosy and Mr. Mot and Sasha (Timothy's girlfriend) and Tommy Geller and Fritz and Mr. Fodder (he's my school lunch guy, remember?). I didn't know they were coming. They just started showing up in ones and twos.

"What are <u>you</u> doing here?" I asked Bee the first time I answered the door.

"Well that's a fine how-do-you-do," she said, "especially since I brought pizza."

And sure enough, behind her stood Mr. Fodder with an armload of pizza boxes from Bee's family's restaurant, Fare.

I led Bee and Mr. Fodder into the kitchen so he could put down the pizza. Mom and Dad and Timothy were standing there smiling at me. Actually, I'd call Timothy's expression more of a smirk. They all had on Hawaii shirts and flower ropes around their necks.

"Nice necklace," I said to Timothy.

IT'S CALLED A *LEI*, DUNDERHEAD.
IT'S A HAWAII THING.

"We're having a
Hawaii party," said
Timothy. "For you. I guess
because you're not a wimp anymore. Or at least
not the wimpiest kid in the world."

Then in came Mr. Mot and
Goosy, who was wearing a skirt
<u>made</u> <u>out</u> <u>of</u> <u>dead</u> <u>weeds</u>.

"You learned how to hula hoop, Aldo,"
said Goosy. "But if you're going to be a Hawaiian
hedonist,* you have to learn how to hula too."

"Oh no. Hornswoggled again."

Mom put a lei around my neck and kissed me
once on each cheek, and the pizza boxes got spread
out on the island (it was Hawaiian pizza, of
course), along with some Hawaiian punch. After
Danny, Tommy, and Fritz showed up, Mr. Mot
brought out a dinky guitar called a ukulele and
played us a few songs while we finished feasting.

DID YOU EVER NOTICE?

FOOD + MUSIC + FRIENDS & FAMILY = A PARTY!

Then the doorbell rang one more time. When I opened the door, there stood a lady-girl with long yellow hair and green glasses. It was totally dark out by now, and the streetlamp made a halo* of light around her head.

"Why hello, Aldo... You might not remember me because we met under some pretty hectic* circumstances. I'm Hazel. I'm the ski patrol person who helped you off the mountain the other day."

IF HAZEL'S HERE, THEN WHO'S HELPING TODAY'S HOTDOGGERS?

"Oh."

"I'm here for the Hawaii party. Fritz invited me."

"Oh."

"I was thinking maybe I could come in..."

"Oh! OK."

So Hazel joined in with us as we all learned how to hula. If you think hula hooping is embarrassing, you should try hula _dancing_. At least my broken arm gave me a good reason to skip the flowery hand motions.

HULA HAND MOTIONS ARE SIGN LANGUAGE WITH STYLE!

A SKIRT YOU CAN MAKE WITH YARD WASTE

After the dance lesson, Mr. Mot played a slideshow on our TV of some of his best Hawaii photos. When that got boring, us non-teenager kids snuck upstairs to our winter fort.

There were more of us than usual, so we really had to huddle* up, especially after Mr. Fodder knocked and asked if he could come in too. He wanted to hear the broken arm story, so Jack and I retold the heroic tale. To keep everyone awake, we might have exaggerated a little, Mr. Krug-style.

"Sounds like hotdogging was hazardous to your health,* hombre,*" said Tommy.

"It was. But to tell you the truth, it was also kinda heart-stopping.* In a good way."

"And you thought January was humdrum, Aldo," said Bee.

You know what? I'm looking forward to some humdrum this weekend. Luckily there are a few days left in January for me to curl up in my cozy house with Maxie by my side and just... hang loose.

"H" GALLERY

Mr. Mot used to be an English teacher. He's a word nerd, and he likes to help me use awesome words in my sketchbooks. I mark the best words with one of these: * (it's called an asterisk). When you see an * you'll know you can look here, in the Gallery, to see what the word means. If you don't know how to say some of the words, just ask Mr. Mot. Or someone you know who's like Mr. Mot. Or go to aldozelnick.com, and we'll say them for you.

H_2O (pg. 19): water, which is 2 hydrogen atoms and 1 oxygen atom stuck together so they look like Mickey Mouse

haberdasher (pg. 62): a guy who sells hats. Yes, that's actually a job.

hack (pg. 23): deal with

haggard (pg. 55): crazy worn-out looking

hair-raising (pg. 105): so scary that the little hairs on your arms and neck stand up

halcyon (pg. 31): like Mr. Mot said, peaceful and calm

half-pint (pg. 60): little kid

halitosis (pg. 49): breath so bad it's a diagnosis

hallucinate (pg. 113): see things that aren't really there

halo (pg. 140): those light-circles angels wear over their heads that mean they're quite a few levels higher than you

halt (pg. 21): a fancy word for stop

handkerchief (pg. 80): a square cloth for sneezing into. Gross. (There's one in my back pocket on page 41.)

handy (pg. 94): useful

hang 10 (pg. 46): stand with your 10 toes hanging over the front of the surfboard, like I'm doing on page 34. (What if you only have 9 toes, like Hercules has 9 fingers? I guess you hang 9?)

hang loose (pg. 47): chillax

hang of it, the (pg. 69): a feel for how to do something

hangers-on (pg. 85): people who want to get in on whatever you're doing because you're cool

harassment (pg. 74): botheringness

harbinger (pg. 130): a sign that something's going to happen; an omen

hardship (pg. 70): something that makes you suffer

hare (pg. 123): Hares are just like rabbits except they're born furry (rabbits are born bald); eat hard food like twigs (rabbits eat soft stuff like leaves); and live above ground (rabbits live in underground tunnels). So hares are also the <u>opposite</u> of rabbits. Weird.

harebrained (pg. 64): super dumb

harmless (pg. 79): wouldn't hurt a mosquito

Harrison, George (pg. 62): the main guitar guy in that famous geezer band called the Beatles. He also wrote lots of songs.

hasty (pg. 41): doing something faster than you should because you'll probably mess up

hat-trick (pg. 49): when the same player gets 3 goals in 1 game

haters gonna hate (pg. 121): a saying that means you're not bothered by people who tease you or say mean things

hazardous to your health (pg. 143): dangerous; hurtful to your body

head-plant (pg. 60): landing head-first in the snow

headquarters (pg. 11): the main place to meet and do important work, like figure out what sketchbook I is going to be called...

headsie (pg. 86): bouncing the ball off your noggin

heart-stopping (pg. 143): so exciting your heart skips a beat or 2

heartbroken (pg. 111): so sad it feels like your heart is cracked in half

heartless (pg. 14): so mean it's like you don't even have a heart

heated (pg. 12): when people are getting mad and worked up

heavy-duty (pg. 18): big and substantial

heavy-hearted (pg. 135): sad

hectic (pg. 140): busy and discombobulating

hedonist (pg. 139): someone who only wants to have fun and relax and never do anything hard. Sign me up!

heebie-jeebies (pg. 22): the creeps; ew-ness

helping (pg. 22): an amount of food that is how much a normal person eats. I usually eat at least 2 helpings. Of anything. Except vegetables.

2 HELPINGS OF THE GOOD STUFF

1 HELPING OF BROCCOLI

hematite (pg. 58): I already told you everything I know about this rock. Ask Jack.

hence (pg. 72): so...

herbivores (pg. 79): a plant-eater

herded (pg. 40): walked close behind in a way that practically pushed me where I was supposed to go

héroe (pg. 49): "hero" in Spanish. *Eres mi héroe* means "You're my hero."

heroic (pg. 57): hero-ish

herring, red (pg. 42): So, a red herring is a kind of fish. But when you say something's a "red herring," it means a distraction from the real thing you should be paying attention to. A "mom-sympathy herring" is a kind of red herring that's especially good at distracting moms.

Hershey, Milton (pg. 62): the guy who started the big chocolate company that makes Hershey's bars and Hershey's Kisses. Like Willy Wonka for reals.

hesitate (pg. 104): wait before you do something because you're scared or not sure

hideousness (pg. 57): hideous means really gross, so hideousness is a state of mega grossness

hieroglyphics (pg. 35): ancient writing in a symbols alphabet

high spirits (pg. 91): happy

high-fiving (pg. 53): putting your hand up in the air and smacking your palm against someone else's

high-tenned (pg. 95): did a high-five except with both hands

highjack (pg. 64): stop someone from going where they were going and take them where you want them to go instead

Hillary, Sir Edmund (pg. 62): the first person to climb to the top of Mount Everest, which is in Nepal and is 29,029 feet tall. I hope he packed a couple hoagies.

hindrance (pg. 110): something that keeps you from doing what you want to do

hip (pg. 29): cool

hirsute (pg. 22): uber hairy

hit the slopes (pg. 7): go skiing

ho-hum (pg. 132): boring

hoagies (pg. 92): a cooler name for sub sandwiches

hoax (pg. 86): trick

hog-wild (pg. 96): really excited and acting crazy about

SQUEE!

hogwash (pg. 74): totally not true

hoisted (pg. 62): lifted up

hold your horses (pg. 107): a saying that means you're being too hasty or harebrained and you should stop and think first

hollered (pg. 52): yelled

hombre (pg. 143): mister (in Spanish)

honeydew (pg. 94): a melon that's green inside and tastes sweet and yummy

honker (pg. 34): a big wave

honor (pg. 28): respect

hoodies (pg. 41): If you're a kid, you know what a hoodie is. Sheesh.

hoodwink (pg. 42): trick

hoopla (pg. 89): something that takes a lot of stuff and work to accomplish

hopeful (pg. 81): full of hope

horchata (pg. 65): Find a recipe at aldozelnick.com

horizontal (pg. 82): flattish side-to-side

hornswoggled (pg. 66): tricked

horrid (pg. 22): awful

hot air (pg. 32): blah, blah, blah

Pssst!

hot springs (pg. 100): warm water that bubbles out of the ground and smells like rotten eggs

hotdogger (pg. 8 and 53): a person who's good at tricky athletic moves and likes to show them off

hotshot (pg. 109): a person who's really good and confident at something, but it can be anything, not just sports

hubbub (pg. 53): excitement

hubris (pg. 75): so much self-confidence that you might do something stupid

huck (pg. 23): throw

huddle (pg. 142): smoosh together in a tight human circle

huevos rancheros (pg. 70): a Mexican breakfast with fried eggs, refried beans, and salsa piled on top of a tortilla

huffy (pg. 26): mad

humdrum (pg. 13): borrring

humiliation (pg. 19): feeling really awkward and embarrassed because other people are noticing something weird or bad that you did

humility (pg. 7): the opposite of hotdoggerness and hotshotness; being humble

Humuhumunukunuku-apua'a (pg. 96): a Hawaiian word that means "fish that grunts like a pig"

hunker down (pg. 7): a saying that means you should be patient and stay where you are, even if it's boring

hunky (pg. 49): a girl word that means handsome

hunky-dory (pg. 120): all good

hurrah, last (pg. 160): one final appearance

hurtle (pg. 43): move with great speed. Sounds the same as "hurdle," which means something that's in your way

hush-hush (pg. 113): secret

husky (pg. 17): a little thick for your height

hustle (pg. 85): hurry-upness

hygiene (pg. 17): a fancy word for cleaning your body, to make it sound medically necessary, which it isn't

hyperbole (pg. 32): exaggeration

hyperspeed (pg. 51): so fast it's got the word hyper in front of it

hysterical (pg. 52): acting all emotional and out of control

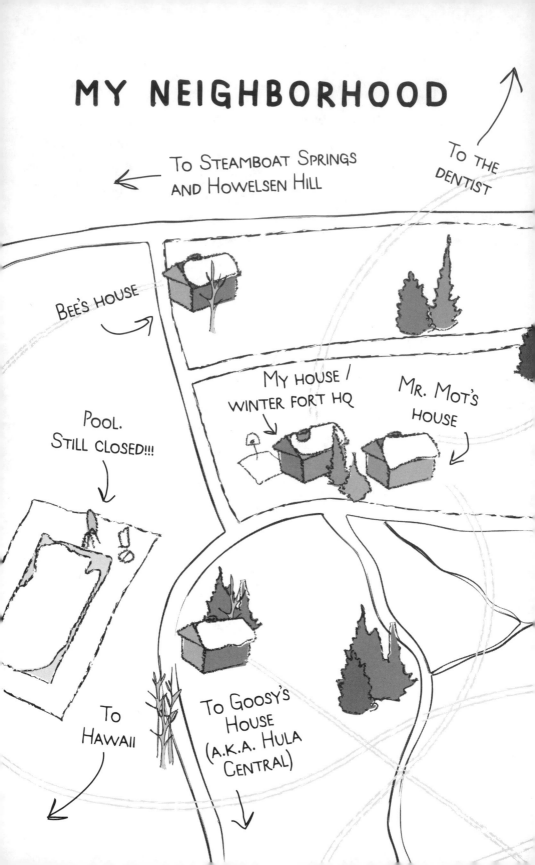

ABOUT THE *award-winning* ALDO ZELNICK COMIC NOVEL SERIES

The Aldo Zelnick comic novels are an alphabetical series for middle-grade readers aged 7-13. Rabid and reluctant readers alike enjoy the intelligent humor and drawings as well as the action-packed stories. They've been called vitamin-fortified *Wimpy Kids*.

NOW AVAILABLE!

160 pages | Hardcover
ISBN: 978-1-934649-04-6
$12.95

Part comic romps, part mysteries, and part sesquipedalian-fests (ask Mr. Mot), they're beloved by parents, teachers, and librarians as much as kids.

Artsy-Fartsy introduces ten-year-old Aldo, the star and narrator of the entire series, who lives with his family in Colorado. He's not athletic like his older brother, he's not a rock hound like his best friend, but he does like bacon. And when his artist grandmother, Goosy, gives him a sketchbook to "record all his artsy-fartsy ideas" during summer vacation, it turns out Aldo is a pretty good cartoonist.

In addition to an engaging cartoon story, each book in the series includes an illustrated glossary of fun and challenging words used throughout the book, such as *absurd, abominable*, and *audacious* in *Artsy-Fartsy* and *brazen, behemoth*, and *boisterous* in *Bogus*.

BAILIWICK PRESS

www.bailiwickpress.com | www.aldozelnick.com

ALSO IN THE ALDO ZELNICK COMIC NOVEL SERIES

ACKNOWLEDGMENTS

"To succeed in life, you need two things: ignorance and confidence."

— Mark Twain

Lucky for Aldo, he has both in spades. And in the rare cases he's lacking in the latter, he manages to muster it somehow.

Here in Karla-and-Kendra Land, we "get" hubris. It's where the gumption to self-sanctify our books for kids comes from—books that are a bit daring and different. But we make them so not to hew to our own whims but because kids deserve funny *and* smart. After all, when it comes to keeping them reading, that very junction is the sweet spot in the Venn diagram of literacy. We hope you agree that the end justifies the means (and that the means are pretty entertaining too).

Yet daily we are humbled by the teachers we meet who are more heroic than Hercules in their work with students; the librarians who devote themselves to putting just the right book into the reluctant reader's hands; the parents from all walks of life who nurture a love for reading in their homes. And then there is our inner circle: Renée, heroic school visit coordinator; the Slow Sanders, handy critiquers; Joe, hotdogger intern; and Launie, hotshot designer. Nor would we fail to honor our families and Aldo's Angels, who hearten us with their unique specialness and support. To all of you, a hearty and heartfelt thanks.

On to I!

ALDO'S HONORABLE ANGELS

Halo There! If you're an Aldo Zelnick fan, e-mail info@bailiwickpress. com and ask for details about becoming an Aldo's Angel. Angels receive special opportunities such as pre-publication discounts, free shipping, naming rights, and listing in the acknowledgments (especially fun for kids).

Barbara Anderson

Carol & Wes Baker

Butch & Sue Byram

Michael & Pam Dobrowski

Leigh Waller Fitschen

Chris Goold

Roy Griffin

Bennett Zent and Calvin, Beckett & Camden Halvorson

Terry & Theresa Harrison

Richard & Peggy Hohm

Vicki & Bill Krug

Papa, Tutu, Cole, Grant, Iris & Thomas Ludwin

Annette & Tom Lynch

Lisa & Kyle Miller

Kristin & Henry Mouton

The Motz & Scripps Families (McCale, Alaina, Caden & Ambria)

Jackie O'Hara & Erin Rogers

Betty Oceanak

Jackie Peterson and Emma, Dorie and Elissa

Slow Sand Writers Society

Dana Spanjer

Vince & Adrianne Tranchitella

THE ALDO ZELNICK FAN CLUB
IS FOR READERS OF ANY AGE WHO
LOVE THE BOOK SERIES AND
WANT THE INSIDE SCOOP ON
ALL THINGS ZELNICKIAN.

GO TO WWW.ALDOZELNICK.COM
AND CLICK ON THIS FLAG-THINGY!

SIGN UP TO RECEIVE:

- sneak preview chapters from the next book.
- an early look at coming book titles, covers, and more.
- opportunities to vote on new character names and other stuff.
- discounts on the books and merchandise.
- a card from Aldo on your birthday (for kids)!

The Aldo Zelnick fan club is free and easy.
If you're under 13, ask your mom or dad to sign you up!

ABOUT THE AUTHOR

Photo by Amy Fesenmaier

Karla Oceanak has been a voracious reader her whole life and a writer and editor for more than twenty years. She has also ghostwritten numerous self-help books. Karla loves doing school visits and speaking to groups about childhood literacy. She lives with her husband, Scott, and their three boys and a cat named Puck in a house strewn with Legos, ping-pong balls, Pokémon cards, video games, books, and dirty socks in Fort Collins, Colorado. This is her eighth novel.

ABOUT THE ILLUSTRATOR

Kendra Spanjer divides her time between being "a writer who illustrates" and "an illustrator who writes." She decided to cultivate her artistic side after discovering that the best part of chemistry class was entertaining her peers (and her professor) with "The Daily Chem Book" comic. Since then, her diverse body of work has appeared in a number of group and solo art shows, book covers, marketing materials, fundraising events, and public places. When she invents spare time for herself to fill, Kendra enjoys skiing, cycling, exploring, discovering new music, watching trains go by, decorating cakes with her sister, making faces in the mirror, and playing with her dog, Puck.